The Mixed-Up Chameleon
by Eric Carle

HarperCollins*Publishers*

Dedicated to all the children who have worked with me on this book.

On a shiny green leaf sat a small green chameleon.
It moved onto a brown tree and turned brownish.
Then it rested on a red flower and turned reddish.
When the chameleon moved slowly across the yellow sand,
it turned yellowish. You could hardly see it.

When the chameleon was warm and had something to eat,
it turned sparkling green.

But when it was cold and hungry,
it turned grey and dull.

When the chameleon was hungry,
it sat still and waited.
Only its eyes moved—up, down, sideways—
until it spotted a fly.
Then the chameleon's long and sticky tongue
shot out and caught the fly.
That was its life.
It was not very exciting.
But one day...

...the chameleon saw a zoo!
It had never seen so many beautiful animals.

The chameleon thought:
How small I am, how slow, how weak!
I wish I could be big and white like a polar bear.
And the chameleon's wish came true.
But was it happy?
No!

I wish I could be handsome like a flamingo.

I wish I could be smart like a fox.

I wish I could swim like a fish.

I wish I could run like a deer.

I wish I could see things far away like a giraffe.

I wish I could hide in a shell like a turtle.

I wish I could be strong like an elephant.

I wish I could be funny like a seal.

I wish I could be like people.
Just then a fly flew by.
The chameleon was very hungry.
But the chameleon was very mixed-up.
It was a little of this and it was a little of that.
And it couldn't catch the fly.

I wish I could be myself.
The chameleon's wish came true.
And it caught the fly!

Sigrid Estrada

Eric Carle says that this book had hundreds of co-authors: the children in many schools in all parts of the United States and Europe where the author-artist has visited. "The children are interested to see how a book is made, the technical aspects, from original drawing to printed page. But I always stress that what is more important than the mechanics of production is the idea, imagination, what-you-feel, what-you-think," says Mr. Carle. Together with the children, he "works" on a book about favorite animals. The children make suggestions. Mr. Carle draws. Requests and instructions come in so fast that there is little time to finish drawing an animal. Only the most characteristic parts are drawn. These parts are then strung together. The more mixed-up the animal becomes, the more hilarious is the audience.

Occasionally, Eric Carle goes to a zoo to sketch the animals from life. Once, watching an iridescent chameleon sitting on a twig, motionless except for its jewellike eyes, he began to wonder, "What if the chameleon could change more than just its color?"

Slowly the experience with the children and the observation of the chameleon merged. The mixed-up chameleon was born.

Eric Carle's name and his signature logotype are trademarks of Eric Carle.

Copyright secured 1975, 1984 in countries signatory to
International Copyright Union. All rights reserved. Manufactured in China.
For information address HarperCollins Children's Books, a division of
HarperCollins Publishers, 195 Broadway, New York, NY 10007.

Library of Congress Cataloging-in-Publication Data
Carle, Eric.
   The mixed-up chameleon.

   Summary: A bored chameleon wishes it could be more
like all the other animals it sees, but soon decides it
would rather be itself.
   [1. Chameleons—Fiction.   2. Self-acceptance—
Fiction.]   I. Title.
PZ7.C21476Mi   1984   [E]   83-45950
ISBN 0-690-04396-1
ISBN 0-690-04397-X (lib. bdg.)

(A Harper Trophy book)
ISBN 0-06-443162-2 (pbk.)

18 SCP 40 39 38 37 36 35 34 33